B.B. THE BEAR

You and Me Make Three was inspired by Michael O'Dea and Mia Johnson,
two great kids who want to help other kids cope with divorce.

To my Dad who's the best Dad in the world,
and to Donny who has been like a father to me.
Michael O'Dea

To all kids who are going through the hard times of divorce.
Mia Johnson

To Mark, for your love and support and for being a wonderful stepfather to Scot and Cari.
E.C.S.

To E.J., you are my rock, to Gwen, Natalie, Joanne, the Schultes and my family, for your love,
and to Dan, for co-parenting with me and maintaining a sense of family for Michael.
W.L.

To my Mi Mi's and Pauly who opened my heart, to Wendy whose friendship knows no bounds
and to Mia's Dad for giving her "Shelia".
G.M.

To Dick, without your love, respect and support, my illustrations would not have been possible. I love you, Baby.
H.D.

Special thanks to EDCO artist, Mark Herrick for his creative talents and assistance with layout and design
and
Lynette Post for her great work and dedication to this B.B. Book and Bear project.

Text copyright ©2008 by Wendy Lokken, Gwendy Mangiamele and Edna Cucksey Stephens
Illustrations copyright ©2008 by Heather Drescher

B.B.'s SMILE Tips For Parents are taken from the SMILE Program and written by Richard S. Victor.

B.B.'s SMILE Tips For Parents and Children's Bill of Rights copyright ©2008 by the SMILE Program
(Start Making It Livable For Everyone). Used by permission.

B.B. the Bear™ is a trademark of Caring Creations, LLC.

Build-A-Bear Workshop® logo is a registered trademark of Build-A-Bear Workshop® - Used by permission

EDCO Publishing, Inc.
2648 Lapeer Road, Auburn Hills, MI 48326
888-510-3326
www.edcopublishing.com

10, 9, 8, 7, 6, 5, 4, 3, 2, 1   ISBN-13: 978-0-9798088-0-7

First Edition - January, 2008   LCCN: 2007939478

Printed in the United States of America by Mitchell Graphics, Petoskey, Michigan

YOU and ME MAKE THREE

B.B. - The Bear Who's Always There Helps Kids With Divorce

Wendy Lokken, Gwendy Mangiamele
and
Edna Cucksey Stephens

Illustrated by Heather Drescher

EDC Publishing Inc.

www.edcopublishing.com

Sometimes kids need a special friend
to talk to when divorce happens in their families.
I'm B.B. the Bear, and I am here to be
your special friend
now that your Mom and Dad
have decided to live in separate homes.

Even though you may not all live in
the same home, both your parents
still love you
just as they always have.
I will be a reminder of how much
your Mom and Dad love you.

When you take me to your Mom's ...

YOU AND ME
MAKE THREE.

And when you take me to your Dad's ...
YOU AND ME
MAKE THREE too!

"HI! I'm B.B.!"

B.B.'s SMILE Tip For Parents

(Start Making It Livable For Everyone)

Divorce is confusing for children. They may be afraid of abandonment or that they will have no place to live. Sometimes children return to, or need security items. Encouraging them to take B.B. or another security item with them to both parents' homes will help provide comfort, security and consistency.

Since I'm your best bear friend, you can whisper in my ear and tell me your biggest secrets.
You can talk to me about how you feel, tell me your silliest jokes and even toss me in the air.
It's good to have a furry friend who is . . .

ALWAYS there!

Wheeee!

B.B.'s SMILE Tip For Parents

In a divorce, every family member must adapt
to a new way of living. Parents should educate
themselves as much as possible about
separation and divorce and how to lessen
the negative impact on children.

When you take me to Mom's, we can play hide and seek, pretend we are riding elephants in the jungle or eat popcorn while we watch our favorite movies.

We can also help Mom by folding laundry and taking out the trash.

There are lots of things we can do with Mom.

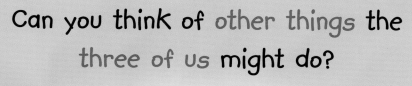

Can you think of other things the three of us might do?

B.B.'s SMILE Tip For Parents

During separation and divorce, parents are trying to cope with changes, increased responsibilities and being on their own. During this same time, children need more affection and attention. It is helpful to make a list of specific activities for together time that both parent and child can enjoy.

At Dad's, we can work and play together too.
We can bake chocolate chip cookies or make mac and cheese.
We can play catch or put a puzzle together, or we could
even build an inside tent!

We can help Dad by
doing the dishes, putting
away the groceries or
raking the leaves.

These are just a few
of many things that you,
Dad and I can do ...
together!

B.B.'s SMILE Tip For Parents

When children have regular routines, they are
less likely to be overwhelmed by the changes
separation brings. In addition to fun activities,
both parents should establish "normal" routines
with chores, bedtime rules, standards for
behavior, and regular meals to help children
feel stable and secure.

And don't forget about homework!
Some things like doing homework, taking baths and brushing teeth
have to be done at both Dad's and Mom's.

I bet you know **other kids** whose parents don't live together.

SCHOO

They spend time with **each parent**
in **different homes** too.
Just like you, these kids
are my friends!

BUS

B.B.'s SMILE Tip For Parents

Parents should approach single parenting with
a positive attitude and speak encouragingly about
the future. They could remind children about other
kids and families who have adjusted to divorce.

Children imitate the behaviors and attitudes
of their parents, their adjustment to divorce
depends on how their parents handle the divorce.

Sometimes kids blame themselves
when their parents don't get along. If you feel something
you said or did is the reason your parents are separating
- DON'T - because it is not your fault and
you should not feel guilty.

B.B.'s SMILE Tip For Parents

Children often feel guilty and blame themselves
for the divorce. Parents should reassure them
that the divorce is not their fault or a
result of anything they have said or done.

Sometimes parents disagree and no matter how hard they try to work things out, they just can't.

That's why they decide it would be better for everyone if they live apart.

And guess what?

Even though
they live apart,
it's O.K.
for you to
love
both your
Mom
and
Dad . . .

just like you did
before
the divorce!

All kids whose parents separate
or divorce have their own feelings
about it.
It's all right to have these feelings.
And it's really, really good
to talk about them.

Think of your feelings as butterflies
locked in a jar waiting to be free.
Once you let the feelings out,
just like the butterflies,
you will feel
so much better!

B.B.'s SMILE Tip For Parents

When divorce occurs, children, as well as parents,
go through a grieving process that includes
feelings of denial, disbelief, anger, sadness,
and depression. Parents should allow children
to express themselves freely. They should listen
and focus on children's feelings without
judging, advising, or teaching.

There are many ways to get your feelings out.

When you feel **lonely** for Dad or Mom,
we could **look** at their picture,
call them on the phone, send an e-mail
or even send them
a secret message in a bottle.

And of course, you can always share your feelings with me because . . .

I'm your best bear friend!

B.B.'s SMILE Tip For Parents

Children miss the parent they are not with and go through an adjustment when getting ready to leave each parent's home. Children should be reassured that it is all right to contact the other parent when they are not together.

Sometimes you might feel worried or afraid.
When you feel this way, hold me close
while you talk to your Mom or Dad.
It's important to share your feelings with each of them.

?

Who will pick me up?

Will I still have my
birthday party?

Where will I sleep?

Where will I keep
my favorite toys?

B.B.'s SMILE Tip For Parents

Children need to know, sometimes over and
over, how they will be affected by the divorce.
They worry about where they will go to school,
where they will live, when they will see the other
parent, friends and relatives. They even worry
about who will take care of them should
something happen to the parent they are with.

When you feel this way, we could
SCREAM
into a pillow . . .

SCREAM!
SCREAM!

GRRRR!

Or we could
make a list and draw pictures
of all the things
that make you ANGRY!

I'll be there
with you no matter
how you feel!

No matter how you are feeling,
the most important thing is to talk about it.

Besides Dad or Mom, you could talk to your
grandparents, favorite teacher or the school counselor.

You might even ask
Mom or Dad
about seeing . . .

someone
who knows about
kids'
feelings
and
divorce.

And of course,
you can always
share your feelings
with me.
I'm a great listener!

B.B.'s SMILE Tip For Parents

Both parents should encourage children to talk to
them about the divorce and their feelings and discuss
problems openly. Questions should be answered
honestly, in terms children can understand.

Children could also be encouraged to talk with people
they trust like grandparents and other relatives,
teachers, psychologists or childcare providers.

Though some things change when parents divorce, many things stay the same...

like how much your Dad and Mom love you.

Other things stay the same too,
like visits to Grandma and Grandpa's,
bedtime stories, birthday parties
and play dates with friends.

Don't Forget your Dentist's Appointment with:

Dr. Phil Matoothe

On: May 17th,

At: 9:00   A.M. / P.M.

B.B.'s SMILE Tip For Parents

Children need continued contact with
friends and relatives of both parents.
It is important to maintain family traditions
as they give children a sense of continuity.

Children crave structure, routine and limits.
They need a predictable, structured home
that makes them feel safe, secure and loved.

You might even find that you have **more friends** and people in your life - some at **Dad's** and some **at Mom's!**

When divorce happens, some things stay **the same** and some things are **different**, but you **still have many, many things** to be **happy** about!

B.B.'s SMILE Tip For Parents

Parents should be sensitive when
introducing new boyfriends or girlfriends
and their families to children.
They often feel confused about their loyalty
and wonder if each parent still loves them as much.
Parents' new relationships may contribute
to their sense of insecurity and instability.

SO SMILE!

Give me a squeeze and remember
both your parents love you
and want you to be happy . . .

and

whether you're at Mom's

or at Dad's

you and me . . .

always
MAKE THREE!

B.B.'s SMILE Tip For Parents

The greatest gift divorced parents can give
their children is to allow them to have a loving,
happy relationship with both parents and not
expose them to continued conflict and hostility.

The second best gift is to make sure they have
a friend like B.B., to love, squeeze
and take to both Dad's and Mom's homes.

SMILE Program's
Children's Bill of Rights

1. The right to be treated as important human beings, with unique feelings, ideas and desires, and not as a source of argument between parents.

2. The right to a continuing relationship with both parents and the freedom to receive love from and express love for both.

3. The right to express love and affection for each parent without having to stifle that love because of fear of disapproval by the other parent.

4. The right to know that their parents' decision to divorce is not their responsibility and that they will continue to be loved by both parents.

5. The right to continuing care and guidance from both parents.

6. The right to honest answers to questions about the changing family relationships.

7. The right to know and appreciate what is good in each parent without one parent degrading the other.

8. The right to have a relaxed, secure relationship with both parents without being placed in a position to manipulate one parent against the other.

9. The right to have both parents not undermine the other parent's time with the children by suggesting tempting alternatives or by threatening to withhold parental contact as a punishment for the children's wrongdoing.

10. The right to experience regular and consistent contact with both parents and to be protected from parental disputes or disagreements.

B.B.

Ink

ABOUT THE AUTHORS

Wendy Lokken, Co-Author

After attending North Dakota State University, Lokken embarked upon a series of highly successful business ventures, most notably as co-owner, broker, president and CEO of **Seatech Realty Inc.** and director of **Seatech Group, Inc.** She also worked with **Borders Books and Music** developing corporate sales initiatives. Lokken is co-owner and secretary of the Board of **Lasertec Inc.**, a nationally renowned processor for electronic statement delivery and high speed print solutions. She is also co-owner of **Caring Creations, LLC** which promotes charitable missions for children through books and education. Lokken has been a **Children International** charity sponsor since 1988. She resides in Naples with her companion, E.J. McDonnell, her son, Michael John O'Dea, II and their dog, Daisy Mae.

Gwendy Mangiamele, Co-Author

With a Bachelor of Science degree in Business Administration from North Dakota State University, Mangiamele has spent the last 20 years working with senior level executives of **Fortune 500** companies, developing national account programs and achieving the distinction of Top Producing Sales and Marketing Executive. She has been featured in Who's Who of Female Executives and is co-owner of **Caring Creations, LLC** which promotes charitable missions for children through books and education. Mangiamele currently resides in Minneapolis with her husband, Paul and daughter, Mia Johnson. She has two grown step-children, P.J. and Megan Mangiamele.

Edna Cucksey Stephens, Co-Author

Founder and President of **EDCO Publishing** in Auburn Hills, Michigan, Cucksey Stephens is the author of children's books, award-winning state curriculums, numerous education newsletters, brochures and white papers. She holds a Bachelor of Arts in Education, a Master's Degree in Reading and Language Arts, as well as a Master's Degree in Special Education from Oakland University. She has an Elementary Administration certification and spent 26 years teaching grades K-college in Lake Orion, Michigan. Stephens has been a Michigan Entrepreneur of the Year finalist and was named Literacy Person of 2005 by the Michigan Reading Association. She is also co-owner of **Caring Creations, LLC** which promotes charitable missions for children through books and education and is co-founder of **International Kids Alliance Network**, a non-profit organization that promotes literacy for children. Stephens resides in Clarkston, Michigan with her husband, Mark. They have two grown children, Scot and Cari Cucksey.

ABOUT THE ILLUSTRATOR

Heather Drescher, Illustrator

Drescher graduated from the Art Institute of Fort Lauderdale with Bachelor of Science degree in Computer Animated Art. She has contributed illustrations to several children's projects including EDCO Publishing's award-winning *L.A.P.'s*™ and *Michigan On The Move* programs, as well as, several endeavors with various authors. She owns *Heather Drescher Artistry*, a business specializing in interior artwork and fine art pieces. She is also co-owner of **Caring Creations, LLC** which promotes charitable missions for children through books and education. Drescher resides in Naples with her companion, Richard Corace, and their dog, Molly.

THE SMILE PROGRAM

The SMILE Program was created in 1989 by the Honorable Edward Sosnick, Judge of the Sixth Judicial Circuit Court, Oakland County, Michigan, and Family Law Attorney, Richard S. Victor, senior partner of the Law Offices of Victor and Victor, PLLC, Bloomfield Hills, Michigan.

The program was designed to help provide education to parents going through divorce so they are better able to understand how to help themselves and their children during a most difficult time in their lives. The underlying theme of SMILE is to teach parents that the greatest gift they can give their children is the right to love the other parent. Through SMILE, parents learn the needs of their children and how they can fill the void, which exists for children when a family faces separation and ultimate divorce. Parents learn that even though they may no longer be marriage partners, they will always be parent partners for their children.

The SMILE Program could not have been possible without the aid and support of the Oakland County, Michigan Friend of the Court and the Family Law Section of the State Bar of Michigan.

SMILE was named by Denise Victor, as a positive acronym for this project, which is now provided, in some form, in every state in the United States and Australia.

A portion of book sales will benefit the VICTOR SMILE FOUNDATION, a non-profit organization created by SMILE Co-founder, Richard S. Victor.

VICTOR SMILE FOUNDATION

"Helping children and parents make the divorce and separation process livable." The mission is to provide education and guidance to children, parents and families, who are going through separation and divorce, in order to help them understand the changes which occur to the family when divorce becomes a life choice for parents. The Foundation will provide support, through its programs and teachings, which will help families, otherwise in dysfunction, learn to cope with each other and how parents can both work together to help their children through this most difficult time in their lives. For more information on the VICTOR SMILE FOUNDATION visit:

www.victorsmilefoundation.org